For my favorite night owl, Justin —A. K. R.
To Sara T, the best owl I know —J. C.

Text © 2008 by Amy Krouse Rosenthal.
Illustrations © 2008 by Jen Corace.

Series design by Kristine Brogno.
Book design by Sara Gillingham.
Typeset in Messcara.
The illustrations in this book were rendered in ink and watercolor.
Manufactured in China.
ISBN 978-0-8118-6023-9

Library of Congress Cataloging-in-Publication Data available.

10 9 8 7 6 5 4 3 2 1

Chronicle Books LLC
680 Second Street, San Francisco, California 94107

www.chroniclekids.com

Little Hoot

by Amy Krouse Rosenthal • illustrated by Jen Corace

chronicle books · san francisco

Once, up on a branch, there was a fellow named Little Hoot.

Little Hoot was a happy little owl.

He liked going to school.

He liked playing hide-n-seek with his forest friends.

He even liked it fine when Mama Owl said it was practice time.

"Time to practice pondering, Sweetie."

"Ok, now practice your staring."

"Staring right,

staring left,

staring right."

But there was one thing Little Hoot did not like:

Bedtime.

Because when you're an owl, you have to stay up late, late, late.

That's just the way it is.

"All my other friends get to go to bed so much earlier than me!

Why do I always have to stay up and play? It's not fair!"

"If you want to grow up to be a wise owl, you must stay up late,"

said Papa Owl.

"And besides, I don't give a hoot what time your friends go to bed.

In this family, we go to bed late. Rules of the roost."

"Stay up and play for one more hour and then you can go to sleep,"
Mama Owl compromised.

"One whole hour?" he boo-whoo'd.
"One whole hour," she cooed.

So off he went.

"When I grow up, I'm going to let my kids go to bed as early as they want."

He played swords.

He played on the jungle gym.

He built a fort.

He jumped in the leaves.

He jumped on the bed.

"Can I stop playing now?" pleaded Little Hoot.

"Ten more minutes of playing, Mister. And please don't ask me again."

"Alright,"
the young owl scowled.

one minute

two minutes

three minutes

four minutes

five minutes

six minutes

seven minutes

eight minutes

nine minutes

ten minutes

"There. I played for one whole hour. *Now* can I go to bed?"

"Yes, now you can go to bed. But . . ."

"Woo-whooooo! Woo-whooooo! Bedtime!!!!!!!!!!!!!!!"

And Little Hoot flew right into bed.

"But wait!" stalled Mama Owl. "What about a bedtime story?"

"And don't forget a glass of water!" added Papa Owl.

But it was too late.

Little Hoot was already fast asleep.

snooze

FIG. 1

snore

FIG. 2

drool

FIG. 3

So they tucked in his feathers.
Gave him a peck on the cheek.

And they owl lived happily ever after. . . .